HEIDI HECKELBECK
Gets Glasses

HEIDI HECKELBECK
and the Secret Admirer

HEIDI HECKELBECK
Is Ready to Dance!

By Wanda Coven
Illustrated by Priscilla Burris

LITTLE SIMON

New York   London   Toronto   Sydney   New Delhi

LITTLE SIMON
An imprint of Simon & Schuster Children's Publishing Division
1230 Avenue of the Americas, New York, New York 10020
This Little Simon bind-up edition July 2015
Heidi Heckelbeck Gets Glasses and *Heidi Heckelbeck and the Secret Admirer* copyright © 2012 by Simon & Schuster, Inc.
Heidi Heckelbeck Is Ready to Dance! copyright © 2013 by Simon & Schuster, Inc.
All rights reserved, including the right of reproduction in whole or in part in any form.
LITTLE SIMON is a registered trademark of Simon & Schuster, Inc., and associated colophon is a trademark of Simon & Schuster, Inc. For information about special discounts for bulk purchases, please contact Simon & Schuster Special Sales at 1-866-506-1949 or business@simonandschuster.com.
The Simon & Schuster Speakers Bureau can bring authors to your live event. For more information or to book an event contact the Simon & Schuster Speakers Bureau at 1-866-248-3049 or visit our website
at www.simonspeakers.com.
Manufactured in the United States of America 0615 MTN
10 9 8 7 6 5 4 3 2 1
ISBN 978-1-4814-5642-5

CONTENTS

CONTENTS

A BRAND-NEW LOOK

Heidi sat at her desk and fiddled with her kitty cat–shaped eraser. *Where's Lucy?* Heidi wondered. Lucy had told her that she had a surprise, and Heidi wanted to be the first to know. She pulled out a strawberry-scented pencil and sharpened it. Heidi looked away for only a moment, and that's exactly when Lucy walked in.

"*Ooh!*" Heidi heard somebody say.

"*Aah!*" said somebody else.

A bunch of kids had already gathered around Lucy. *It must be something important,* thought Heidi. She rushed to the door and wiggled her way into the middle of the crowd.

"Surprise!" said Lucy when she saw Heidi.

"Wow!" Heidi said.

"Wow, *what*?" asked Charlie Chen, who had just walked into the classroom.

"Lucy got glasses!" shouted Heidi.

Lucy's glasses had brown frames with pink sparkly flowers at the temples.

"Wait—let me see!" said Melanie Maplethorpe, pushing her way to the front. Melanie must have liked Lucy's glasses, because she didn't say "Ew" or anything else like that.

"They make you look smart," said Stanley Stonewrecker.

"They make you look hip!" said Natalie Newman.

"They make us look like twins!" said Bruce Bickerson, who also wore glasses.

Lucy and Bruce slapped each other five.

Lucky Lucy, thought Heidi. *She's getting so much attention for her new glasses.* Heidi had to admit, Lucy's glasses were really, really cool.

Mrs. Welli clapped her hands as she walked into the classroom. "Please take your seats, boys and girls!"

Everyone scrambled to their desks.

Mrs. Welli noticed Lucy's glasses right away.

"So stylish, Lucy," Mrs. Welli said. "And now you'll be able to see the chalkboard."

"Thanks," Lucy said with a smile.

All day everyone made a big deal about Lucy's glasses.

During English, Mrs. Welli read from a book of poems. Then she asked everyone to write their own. At the end of class Mrs. Welli asked Lucy to read hers out loud. Heidi knew why Lucy got picked. It was because of her new glasses.

Lucy stood in front of the class and pushed her glasses to the top of her nose.

"'Glasses,'" said Lucy. "By Lucy Lancaster."

"With my brand-new glasses,
I can see so far away.
I see my friends and
teachers
on the playground clear as
day.
The board's no longer blurry—
even if I'm in the last row!

And what's best about my glasses is–
  I've got a brand-new look to show!"

Everyone clapped and whistled.

Lucy curtsied and returned to her seat.

In art, Lucy got the same kind of
attention. Mr. Doodlebee even drew a
picture of Lucy with her glasses and
hung it on the bulletin board.

I wish Mr. Doodlebee would draw a picture of me, thought Heidi. *The problem is, I don't stand out. I need a new look. . . .*

Heidi smiled to herself. *Aha! I know just how to get one.*

FUZZY WUZZY

Heidi stood on top of a chair in the kitchen.

"News alert! News alert!" she said.

"What's the story?" Henry asked.

"I want to get glasses!" said Heidi.

"And I want you to get off that chair before you get hurt," said Mom.

Heidi stepped down from the chair.

"But I *really* want glasses," Heidi said.

"How about you have a snack first?" suggested Mom. She placed a plate of maple granola bars and two glasses of milk on the table.

Heidi and Henry dipped their granola bars in the milk.

"So, why on earth do you want glasses?" Mom asked.

"'Cause they're COOL!" said Heidi.

"Glasses help people see," said Mom. "They're not used to make people look cool."

"Movie stars wear sunglasses, and

THEY look cool," Henry said.

"Movie stars wear sunglasses so people won't know who they really are," said Mom.

"AND to make them look COOL!" said Heidi.

Mom sighed.

"Okay, glasses can also make you look cool," said Mom.

"So can I get some?" Heidi asked.

"No," said Mom. "If you want to look cool, wear your beach glasses."

"But my beach glasses are shaped like hearts," said Heidi. "They'll make me look like a five-year-old."

"Hey!" Henry said. "I'm five and I

wouldn't wear those beach glasses if you paid me!"

"See?" said Heidi. "Even Henry knows what's cool."

"Heidi, you're *not* getting glasses," Mom said.

"I have an idea," said Henry. "You can have MY glasses!"

Heidi rolled her eyes—as if her kid brother would have anything she'd actually want.

Henry ran upstairs and came back with a pair of glasses and a hand mirror.

"Try these," said Henry. "I got them at that 3-D dinosaur movie."

"Where are the lenses?" asked Heidi.

"I took them out," Henry said. "You can't see anything with them in— unless you're at the movies."

Heidi put on the glasses.

"Wow," said Henry. "They make you look super-smart!"

"They look kind of clunky," Heidi said, looking in the mirror.

"Well, you're not going to get glasses unless you really need them," said Mom.

"But I DO need them!" Heidi said. "I have six GREAT reasons why I need glasses."

Heidi held up a finger for each reason. "Number one: Glasses will make me look smarter! Number two: Glasses will help me get more friends! Number three: Glasses will help me read poetry better!"

Mom began to empty the dish-washer. She didn't seem interested in Heidi's Six Great Reasons.

"Number four: I'll get my picture on the art room bulletin board! Number five: Glasses will make me look cool! And number six: Glasses will help me see better, because the thing is, I'm having a little trouble seeing."

Mom frowned. "Maybe what you need is an eye test," she said.

"I'll do it," said Henry. He held up two fingers. "How many fingers do I have?"

Heidi squinted. "Nine . . . uh, wait— ten."

"RIGHT!" said Henry, holding up

both his hands. "I DO have ten fingers! But the answer is TWO. I'm afraid you failed the eye test."

That gave Heidi an idea. *Maybe if I pretend to have bad eyesight, then I can score a pair of super-cool glasses!*

Chapter 3

CUCKOO!

Click!

Mrs. Welli snapped a picture of Lucy in her new glasses.

Mrs. Welli always took pictures when something *big* happened. She hung them on a special bulletin board called "The Wall of Fame." All the photos were of kids with missing teeth, except the one of Stanley with a cast on his arm. Heidi had never made the Wall of Fame. But she planned to—very soon.

"All eyes on the chalkboard!" said Mrs. Welli. "This morning we're going to make compound words. We'll put two words together to form one new word. She wrote the first example on the board.

"The words 'class' and 'room' become 'classroom,'" said Mrs. Welli.

Heidi raised her hand.

"Yes, Heidi," Mrs. Welli said.

"Would you please write the words a little bigger?" asked Heidi. "I can't see them from here."

Mrs. Welli wrote the word "cat" in bigger letters on the board. "Can you read this?" she asked.

Heidi squinted and tried to read the word.

"'Car'?" she said, pretending she couldn't see very well.

Everyone giggled.

Then Mrs. Welli wrote the word "nip" in slightly bigger letters on the board. "Try this one."

"'Nap'?" Heidi asked.

The class laughed harder.

"Come see me after school," said Mrs. Welli.

At the end of the day Heidi went to see her teacher. Mrs. Welli had written a note for Heidi's parents.

"Heidi, this is very important," Mrs. Welli said. "I want you to give this letter to your mother and father when you get home."

Heidi nodded. Then she skipped all the way to the bus. *YES!* Heidi said to herself. *I fooled my teacher! Now all I have to do is fool Mom and Dad—and*

maybe an eye doctor. Then I can get a
cool pair of glasses!

When she got home from school,
Heidi gave the note to her mom. By
dinner her parents had made Heidi
an eye appointment for the next day
after school.

"Uh-oh," said Henry. "Doctors give much harder eye tests than I do."

"Dr. Chen is nice," Mom said. "Heidi, isn't his son, Charlie, in your class?"

Heidi hadn't heard a word of the conversation. She was daydreaming about how she would look in her new glasses.

"Heidi?" said Mom.

"Anybody home?" Dad asked.

"Have you gone deaf, too?" asked Henry.

"Sure," Heidi said dreamily. "I'd love some more potatoes."

Henry shook his head. "She's not blind OR deaf," he said. "She's just plain CUCKOO!"

Chapter 4

EYE CANDY!

"Have a seat," said Dr. Chen.

Dr. Chen had large ears and spiky black hair. Heidi recognized him from school. Today he looked more like a doctor than a dad. He had on glasses with black frames and wore a white lab coat.

Heidi and her mom sat down.

"Heidi, how long have your eyes been bothering you?" Dr. Chen asked.

Heidi tried not to make her story sound too fishy. "I've been seeing fuzzy for a while," she said. "But it really began to bother me a few days ago."

Dr. Chen nodded. "Well, let's take a look," he said.

First, Heidi had to read an eye chart. Dr. Chen gave her something that looked like a black plastic lollipop and asked her to cover one eye with it.

"Now please read line four," said Dr. Chen.

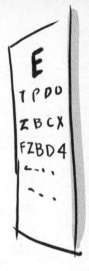

Heidi saw four letters and a number—F Z B D 4—but she didn't read them that way.

"Uh . . . *E, S, R, O,* seven," Heidi said. Dr. Chen looked puzzled. He asked Heidi to read two more lines. She covered the other eye and did the same thing. *I better not read them ALL wrong,* thought Heidi, *or Dr. Chen will think I've gone completely blind.*

Then Dr. Chen shined a light in Heidi's eyes. He told her to look up and down and from side to side.

Next he asked her to peek into what looked like a viewfinder.

Heidi liked viewfinders. She had tried one on a family camping trip.

Her family had hiked up a mountain, and Heidi had spotted a viewfinder at the top. Dad had given her quarters to put inside. She had spied villages, lakes, and churches from up high.

But inside Dr. Chen's viewfinder, Heidi only saw a bunch of letters. Dr. Chen fiddled with the viewfinder and asked Heidi if the letters looked better or worse. Heidi would answer

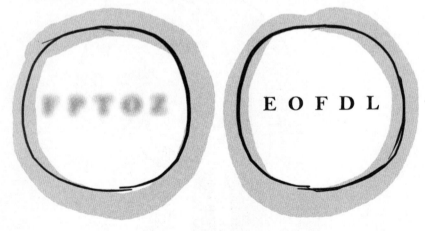

"worse" when the letters looked better and "better" when the letters looked worse. Soon the tests were over.

"Well, Heidi," said Dr. Chen, "it looks like you're going to need glasses."

"That's great news!" Heidi said.

"I'm glad you feel that way," said Dr. Chen.

Dr. Chen took Heidi to the next room. There were racks and racks

of brightly colored glasses. *It's like a candy store!* thought Heidi. *Only better!* She chose a pair of black glasses with glitter inside the plastic— like sparkly gems inside a rock. She tried them on.

"Super-funky," said Heidi, looking in the mirror. Then she turned to her

mom. "What do you think?"

"They're very *you*," said Mom, who
still couldn't get used to the idea that
Heidi needed glasses.

The lady behind the counter told
Heidi she was going to get her new

glasses ready. While she waited, Heidi did a connect-the-dots puzzle, four hidden pictures, and two word searches. It felt like she had been waiting forever, when suddenly . . .

"Heidi Heckelbeck?" called the lady from behind the counter.

Heidi jumped up from her seat.

Finally! she thought. *I can't wait to wear my new glasses. They're going to make me look SO cool.* But when Heidi put them on, she discovered that there was a teeny-weeny problem.

She couldn't see a thing.

Chapter 5

SCOOPS

Heidi took off her glasses on the way to the car. *These glasses are hurting my eyes,* she thought. *Maybe I shouldn't have lied so much about the lines on the eye chart.*

"Put your glasses back on," said Mom. "You need to wear them in order to get used to them."

Heidi listened to her mom and put them back on. She slid them a little way down her nose. *That's better. Now I can see over the top.*

"No cheating," said Mom.

"Okay," said Heidi as she slid the glasses back in place.

Mom pulled into a shopping plaza

and parked in front of Scoops—Heidi's favorite ice-cream shop.

"Surprise!" said Mom. "I thought we would celebrate your new glasses with ice cream."

Heidi saw Dad and Henry waving from inside the shop.

"Thanks, Mom!" said Heidi.

She hopped out of the car and lifted her glasses so she wouldn't trip on the curb. Then she put them back in place when she got inside.

Dad patted Heidi on the back.

"You look so grown-up," Dad said.

"You look more like you're playing dress-up," said Henry.

"Very funny," Heidi said. "But these are the REAL thing."

Heidi handed her glasses to Henry, and he put them on.

"Whoa!" said Henry. "I can't see a thing!"

"I told you I needed glasses," said Heidi as she put them back on.

Then they went to order ice cream.

"What can I get for you?" asked a girl in a Scoops T-shirt.

Heidi looked at the menu on the back wall. She couldn't read any of the flavors, and she couldn't sneak a

peek from under her glasses because her whole family was watching.

"I'll try a scoop of that one," Heidi said, pointing to the special of the day.

"I'll have Moose Tracks," said Henry.

After they got their cones, Dad grabbed napkins and they headed outside.

Heidi took a lick of her cone. "Ew!" she said. "It tastes like pineapple."

"Duh," Henry said. "Because that's what you ordered."

Merg, thought Heidi. But she didn't make a big deal about ordering the wrong ice cream. She didn't want her family to wonder what was wrong with her glasses. Heidi looked for a

wastebasket to pitch her cone into,
and then . . . *bonk!* She bumped
into Henry and—*squash!*—his cone
smushed right into his nose.

Henry began to whine.

"I'm sorry, little buddy. I didn't

mean to," said Heidi. "Here, you can have mine."

Heidi offered her cone to Henry, but he pushed it away. She shrugged and tossed her cone in the trash.

"What a fiasco!" said Mom as she wiped ice cream off Henry's face.

"What's that mean?" asked Henry.

"It means that this ice-cream trip almost turned into a disaster," said Dad.

Heidi began to wonder if her new glasses might be a fiasco too, but she pushed that thought right out of her head.

Chapter 6

WHAT A KLUTZ!

The next morning Heidi made a grand entrance at school.

"*One! Two! Three!*" she counted.

Then she burst into the classroom.

Nobody looked.

"AHEM," said Heidi as she made her way toward her desk.

Still nobody looked—until . . .

Whump! Heidi bumped smack into Melanie. Melanie's armful of books tumbled to the floor.

"Hey! Watch where you're going, weirdo!" Melanie said.

"Uh, sorry," said Heidi. "I'm still getting used to my new glasses."

Heidi helped Melanie pick up her books.

"Since when do YOU wear glasses?" Melanie asked.

"Since yesterday," said Heidi. "So, what do you think?"

Melanie took a close look at Heidi.

"Black is not a good color for you," said Melanie. "But I like the sparkles."

Coming from Melanie, that was a compliment.

"Thanks," said Heidi, before she continued on to her desk.

Then—*bonk!*—Heidi crashed into her chair and knocked it over. It clanked on the floor. This time everyone looked. *Finally!* thought Heidi as she picked up her chair. Lucy and Bruce ran to Heidi's desk.

"You got glasses!" Lucy said.

"Why didn't you tell us?" asked Bruce.

"I didn't find out until yesterday that I was getting them," explained Heidi. "Do you like them?"

"I love them!" said Lucy.

"They're super-cool," Bruce said.

"Thanks," said Heidi. "Now we can be triplets!"

Heidi, Lucy, and Bruce high-fived. Heidi mostly slapped air because everything was so fuzzy.

Everyone swarmed around Heidi until Mrs. Welli asked the class to take their seats.

"Heidi, your glasses look lovely," said Mrs. Welli. "Come see me during snack time, and I'll take your picture."

Heidi nodded.

That means I'm going to make the Wall of Fame! thought Heidi. She felt so important. The only problem was, she couldn't see much with her new glasses.

When Heidi wrote in her journal, her sentences came out slanted. In art, the class had to draw a bowl of fruit. Heidi's looked more like a bowl of garbage.

My glasses help me see better.

"Why did you paint red bananas and purple apples?" asked Lucy.

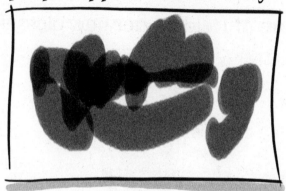

"Those are bananas?" Bruce asked.

"Mr. Doodlebee called it 'artistic interpretation,'" said Heidi.

"What's that?" Lucy asked.

"It means that the artist has completely lost her marbles," replied Melanie.

Heidi covered her ears to drown out

the laughter. To make matters worse, Mr. Doodlebee didn't even draw a picture of Heidi in her new glasses.

At lunch Heidi bumped into the table with her tray. She took off her glasses so she could wipe up the juice that had spilled all over.

"Are you *sure* you need glasses?" questioned Lucy.

Heidi shoved her glasses back on. "Of course I'm sure," she said. "I'm just getting used to them."

"Mine felt good on the very first day," said Lucy.

"Well, lucky for you!" said Heidi.

Lucy and Bruce gave each other a look. Heidi pretended not to notice.

At dinner that night Heidi poured milk all over the floor.

"You're such a klutz!" said Henry.

"Am not!"

"Are too!"

"Enough," said Dad.

"Heidi," said Mom, "are your new glasses bothering you?"

"No," lied Heidi. "I love them."

But the truth was, Heidi's eyeballs were killing her. She skipped dessert and went to her room. That night Heidi fell sound asleep in her tights, shoes, clothes—everything except her glasses, which had fallen on the floor.

Chapter 7

BiRD BREW

Heidi peeked out from under her covers. Had she dreamed she had gotten glasses? No such luck. There they were on her bedside table. Someone had picked them up during the night.

Then Heidi's door burst open.

"Race you downstairs!" shouted Henry. "Dad made apple fritters for Saturday breakfast."

Heidi pulled the sheet over her head. Henry was too loud, too happy, and way too awake for her. *But since it's Saturday,* she thought, *I get to visit Aunt Trudy.* Heidi loved her aunt Trudy. She taught Heidi spells and showed her how to use her gifts as a witch.

Heidi got out of bed and got ready for the day. After brushing her teeth, she put on her black jeans and her I ♥ BABY ANIMALS T-shirt. Then she trotted downstairs with her glasses in her pocket.

"I'm off to Aunt Trudy's," Heidi said as she grabbed an apple fritter.

"Be back for lunch," said Mom. "Remember, Lucy's coming over. And don't forget to wear your glasses."

Heidi nodded. On her way to Aunt Trudy's she nibbled her apple fritter and kicked an acorn along the sidewalk. *It sure is nice to be able to see,* Heidi thought. When she got to Aunt Trudy's, she put on her glasses and rang the bell.

"Oh my," said Aunt Trudy as

she opened the door. "Don't *you* look smart!"

Aunt Trudy gave Heidi a big hug. Her aunt smelled like flowers— because she had her own perfume business. Heidi followed Aunt Trudy into the kitchen. She peeked out from under her glasses so she wouldn't trip.

"You know what's odd?" asked Aunt Trudy.

"What?" Heidi said.

"None of the witches in our family have ever needed glasses. I mean, sometimes I use magnifying glasses to read very fine print, but that's not the same as real glasses."

Heidi shrugged, then changed the subject. "What are these?" she asked, picking up one of the little bottles on the kitchen table.

"Those bottles are for Percy," said
Aunt Trudy.

Percy was Aunt Trudy's beloved
parrot. Most of his feathers were
bright red, and his wings were yellow
and blue.

"Is Percy okay?" Heidi asked.

"I'm afraid he's under the weather," said Aunt Trudy. "Would you like to mix him a get-well potion?"

"Would I ever!" said Heidi.

"Then let's get right to work," said Aunt Trudy.

She opened her *Book of Spells* and placed it in front of Heidi.

Heidi did her best to figure out the words with her glasses on. "Bird stew?" she asked uncertainly.

Aunt Trudy laughed. "No, silly.

We're going to make Percy a get-well
brew."

"Oh—I see," Heidi said.

"Well, I should hope so, with those
fancy new glasses!" said Aunt Trudy.

Chapter 8

BiRDBRAiN

Aunt Trudy lifted Percy out of his cage and set him on his perch. Heidi measured the ingredients.

Three tablespoons of pepper, Heidi read to herself—or at least, that's what she thought she read. Heidi measured three tablespoons of pepper and dumped them in the bowl. She tried to read the next ingredient. *Eight*

tablespoons of ground sunflower seeds—or is that a three? Heidi wondered. *No, it looks more like an eight.* She added the seeds to the mix and looked at the next item. *A half cup of maple syrup.* Heidi poured the maple syrup into the mix and stirred it together.

"The brew's ready," Heidi said.

"Good work," said Aunt Trudy.

Aunt Trudy picked up the bowl and brushed the brew on Percy's feathers. Then she held her Witches of Westwick medallion in her left hand and placed her right hand over Percy.

She chanted the words of the spell.

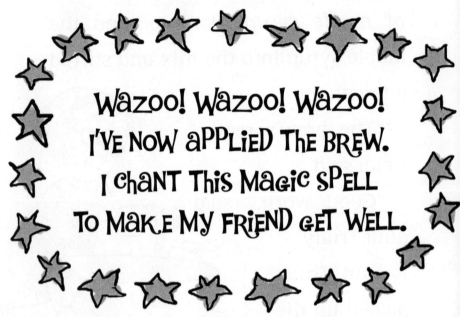

Wazoo! Wazoo! Wazoo!
I've now applied the brew.
I chant this magic spell
To make my friend get well.

Percy ruffled his feathers and squawked.

"Are you feeling better, sweet boy?" asked Aunt Trudy.

Percy squawked again.

Then something odd happened.

Percy began to grow.

He grew and grew and GREW.

Crack!

Percy's perch snapped in two, and he kept on growing.

He became the size of a cat.

Then the size of a dog. Soon he was as

large as a pony.

"Oh, goodness me!" Aunt Trudy cried nervously.

"What's happening?" asked Heidi.

"It seems that something's gone wrong with our

get-well brew," said Aunt Trudy. She grabbed the *Book of Spells* and began to read the ingredients out loud.

"Eight tablespoons of pepper . . ."

"No, three," corrected Heidi.

"And three tablespoons of ground sunflower seeds . . ."

"No, eight," Heidi said.

Aunt Trudy handed the book to Heidi and folded her arms. Heidi took off her glasses and read the ingredients. She had mistaken the number three for the number eight and the number eight for the number three. *Oh no,* thought Heidi. *I totally blew it.*

"*Br-r-r-r-ock!*" squawked Percy, whose head now touched the ceiling.

Chapter 9

DUMB AND DUMBER

Heidi felt like a complete birdbrain.
Percy was the size of an elephant.
Aunt Trudy was afraid he might grow
even more and burst through the roof.
She had to reverse the spell—and fast.
Aunt Trudy held her medallion in her
left hand and chanted:

WAZOO! WAZOO! WAZEE!
PLEASE LET THIS BIRD BE FREE!
WE MADE A BLUNDER —
MOST UNWISE.
NOW MAKE THIS BIRD
A NORMAL SIZE!

Swoosh! A great gust of wind swirled around Percy.

"B-r-r-r—ock!" he squawked.

Heidi covered her eyes. Some of the potion bottles on the table clinked and fell over. Then it became quiet.

"You can look," Aunt Trudy said.

Heidi peeked between her fingers. Percy was sitting on the kitchen table. He was just the right size for a parrot. Heidi stroked his head with her finger.

"I'm glad he didn't go through the roof," said Heidi.

"Me too," said Aunt Trudy. "But he still needs the bird brew treatment."

Heidi whipped up another batch of the bird brew and brushed it on Percy. This time she didn't wear her glasses, and this time Heidi chanted the spell herself. *I hope it works,* she thought.

When she had finished chanting, she looked at Percy.

Percy fluffed his feathers and flew onto Heidi's shoulder.

"He's nuzzling my hair," said Heidi.

"That's his way of saying thank you," said Aunt Trudy.

Heidi and Aunt Trudy laughed.

Then Aunt Trudy picked up Heidi's glasses. "So what's the story behind these?" she asked.

Heidi bit her lip. "The story is . . . ," Heidi began. "The story is . . . I never really needed glasses."

"I *knew* it!" said Aunt Trudy. "None of the Witches of Westwick have ever

needed glasses." Then she looked into Heidi's eyes. "So what's the *rest* of the story?"

"I wanted to be cool," Heidi said.

Aunt Trudy laughed.

"What's so funny?" asked Heidi.

"It reminds me of when I was your age," said Aunt Trudy. "I wanted to be cool too, so one time I wore a strip of tinfoil on my top teeth for a whole day."

"Why?"

"Because I thought braces were cool."

"So you made fake braces out of tinfoil?" Heidi asked.

"That's right," said Aunt Trudy.

Heidi laughed. "That's even dumber than what I did!"

"Well, I'd say it's more of a tie," said Aunt Trudy with a wink.

"Yeah, maybe," Heidi said.

"And let's be thankful we don't need glasses *or* braces," said Aunt Trudy. "And above all, remember this. . . ."

"What?"

"That you already are a very special girl. Just think—how many girls have special powers like you?"

"None that I know of," said Heidi.

Aunt Trudy gave Heidi a big hug. Then Heidi shoved her glasses into her pocket and skipped all the way home for lunch.

BONKERS!

"Heiii-diii!" called Dad from the back door. "Lucy's here!"

Heidi and Henry had just found four rocks to hold down the corners of the tablecloth on the picnic table. They put the rocks in place and ran to the house.

"The picnic food is all ready," said Dad.

Heidi carried a platter of sandwiches. Lucy carried the brownies. Henry got the chips. Dad grabbed two bottles of his homemade fizzy lemonade, and Mom brought plates, napkins, and cups.

They all sat at the picnic table
under the shade of a maple tree.

"Everything looks so good!" said Heidi.

"How do you know?" asked Henry. "You're not wearing your glasses."

"Who needs glasses?" Heidi asked. Everyone stared at Heidi.

"What do you mean?" asked Lucy.

"Well, the truth is," said Heidi. "I don't really *need* glasses."

"You're kidding!" said Dad.

"I wondered!" said Mom.

"I KNEW it!" said Henry.

"So why'd you get them?" asked Lucy.

"Because I wanted to be cool, like you and Bruce," Heidi said.

"Wow—you must be CRAZY!" said Lucy. "Because I wish I *didn't* need glasses."

"No, YOU'RE crazy!" said Heidi.
"Because glasses look really good on
you."

"You know what?" Henry said.
"You're BOTH crazy!"

"That means we must be TWINS!"
said Heidi.

Heidi and Lucy slapped each other
five.

Henry rolled his eyes. "See what I mean? TOTALLY bonkers."

"Heidi may be a little bonkers," said Dad, "but she's also very special."

"It's true," said Mom, giving Heidi a hug. "You don't need glasses to make you more special. We love you just the way you are."

CONTENTS

Chapter 1

HOWDY, PARTNER!

Heidi Heckelbeck couldn't wait for the Brewster second-grade science fair. Science experiments were the next best thing to mixing magic potions.

"We find out our science partners today," said Heidi as she and Bruce Bickerson bounced along in their seat at the back of the school bus. "I hope I don't get Melanie Maplethorpe."

"Same here," Bruce said. "I wouldn't want to get her best friend, Stanley Stonewrecker, either."

"Make a fist for good luck," said Heidi.

They both made a fist.

"Pound it," said Heidi.

Bruce pounded his knuckles with Heidi's.

But it didn't seem to do any good.

When their teacher, Mrs. Welli, announced science partners, Heidi got Stanley and Bruce got Melanie.

"Poor thing," said Lucy Lancaster, who had gotten Charlie Chen.

"You're lucky you got Charlie," said Heidi. "He's nice AND smart."

Mrs. Welli asked everyone to sit with his or her partner. Heidi didn't

budge. *I'd rather sit next to an egg-salad sandwich than Stanley Stonewrecker,* she thought. Stanley set his chair next to Heidi's and sat down. Heidi wanted to stick her tongue out at him, but she didn't.

"Now it's time to pick a science experiment," said Mrs. Welli. "I have a list to choose from—or you can come up with your own."

She handed a stack of papers to Melanie to pass out.

"You have two days to choose an experiment," Mrs. Welli said. "The science fair is the following Saturday. Be ready to show your experiment to the judges. You'll also need to explain what happened and why on note cards."

Melanie dropped the list of science experiments on Heidi's desk.

"I'll bet you were behind all this, weren't you?" asked Melanie.

"Behind all what?" asked Heidi.

"Behind you getting my best friend for a partner and me getting your ding-dong friend," Melanie said.

"I'd say it pretty much stinks for all of us," said Heidi.

"Well, at least for once we agree on something," said Melanie.

Chapter 2

MOTHBALLS

The next day in class Heidi and Stanley flipped through the list of science experiments.

"How about a volcano?" suggested Heidi.

"That sounds cool," Stanley said. "Let's do it."

Well, that was easy, thought Heidi. She began to write "volcano" on a piece of paper to give Mrs. Welli.

Then Melanie raised her hand.

"Yes, Melanie?" said Mrs. Welli.

"Bruce and I would like to make a volcano for the science fair," said Melanie. She had overheard Heidi and Stanley talking!

"Uh . . . we *do*?" questioned Bruce.

"I thought we were going to make a shoe-box maze."

Melanie elbowed Bruce. "Play along, dum-dum," she whispered.

"Okay," Mrs. Welli said. "I'll put you down for a volcano."

Melanie turned around and made a mean face at Heidi.

Heidi pounded her fist on the desk.

"Shush," Stanley said. "We'll get in trouble."

"But she stole our idea!" said Heidi.

"We'll just have to come up with something better," said Stanley.

"Like what?" Heidi asked.

"I dunno," said Stanley. "Let's take another look."

Stanley flipped through a few

more experiments. He found a magic ketchup and an exploding lunch bag project. But nothing sounded as good as a volcano. Then Stanley remembered something he'd seen on TV.

"How about dancing mothballs?" said Stanley. "Mothballs dance when you add water and other stuff to them."

Heidi knew all about mothballs. Her grandma Mabel stored her woolens with mothballs every summer to keep away the moths. Heidi remembered how some of her grandma's sweaters would smell like mothballs even after they were no longer stored with them.

"I guess so," Heidi said.

Stanley raised his hand.

"Heidi and I would like to do dancing mothballs," said Stanley.

"Very good," said Mrs. Welli, writing it down.

"So now what?" Heidi asked.

"We need to learn more about our experiment," said Stanley.

"My dad's a soda-pop scientist," Heidi said. "Maybe he can help us. Do you want to come over after school?"

"Sure," said Stanley.

Whoa, I can't believe I just asked Stanley Stonewrecker to come over to my house, thought Heidi.

Well, it wasn't like this made him her friend or anything.

Chapter 3

RAiSiNS

Ding-dong!

"I'll get it!" said Heidi as she thundered down the stairs.

Heidi met her mom and little brother, Henry, in the front hall.

"Who is it?" asked Henry.

Heidi put a finger to her lips and

whispered, "Shh . . . It's Stanley."

"SMELL-A-NIE'S Stanley?" asked Henry.

"*Shush!* He's going to hear you," Heidi whispered.

"But what's he doing here?" asked Henry.

"The two of us are working on a science project," whispered Heidi.

Ding-dong!

"Coming!" Heidi called.

"And you picked Stanley?" asked Henry.

"Of course not!" Heidi whispered loudly. "My TEACHER picked him."

"Yikes!" whispered Henry as Mom scooted him away from the door.

Heidi brought Stanley into the kitchen. "Stanley, this is my mom and my little brother, Henry," she said.

"Hi, Stanley," said Mom. "Would you like a Rice Krispies bar?"

Stanley said yes and helped himself

to one. He saw Henry pull a Candy Pop from a kitchen drawer. Henry tore off the wrapper and popped the candy into his mouth.

"That better not be the last one," Heidi said.

"It's not," said Henry. "We have five left."

"What flavors?" asked Heidi.

"Coconut," said Henry.

"What else?" Heidi asked.

Henry peeked in the candy drawer.

"More coconut," he said.

"What happened to all the grape ones?" Heidi asked.

"Maybe they got stolen," said Henry.

"Is the thief, by any chance, named HENRY?" asked Heidi.

Henry pulled the Candy Pop out of

his mouth, followed by a slimy trail of purple spit. "Want the rest of this one?" he asked.

"That's gross," Heidi said.

Henry shrugged.

Just then the back door banged open. Mr. Heckelbeck was home! He walked in and set a bag of groceries on the counter.

"The gang's all here!" said Dad cheerfully.

He introduced himself to Stanley.

"We're partners in the science fair,"

said Heidi as Dad kissed the top of her
head.

"Our project is dancing mothballs,"
said Stanley.

"Need some help?" Dad asked.

"Yeah!" said Heidi.

"Definitely," said Stanley.

"Okay, here's what you'll need,"
said Dad.

Heidi got a sheet of paper and a

pencil from the kitchen desk. "Ready," she said.

"You'll need water, vinegar, baking soda, and mothballs," Dad said.

Heidi wrote everything down.

"It works with raisins, too," said Dad.

"Ooh! Let's use raisins!" said Heidi.

Stanley agreed.

Heidi wanted to do the experiment right away, but Dad had to work on a new cola.

"Let's meet here tomorrow after school," Dad suggested. "We'll run the experiment from my home lab."

"Sounds like a plan!" Heidi said. "I'll get what we need for the experiment. Stanley, you can gather the note cards and art supplies for our poster."

Dad held his hand in the air, and Heidi and Stanley high-fived it.

So far, so good, Heidi thought.

Chapter 4

STiNKBUG

The next morning Heidi rounded
up everything they would need for
the science experiment. She found
an empty fishbowl in the kitchen
cupboard. It was round and fat like a
globe. *This will be perfect to show off
our dancing raisins,* thought Heidi.

She took a big box of raisins from the pantry as well as the baking soda and vinegar. Heidi put all the items in a brown paper bag and kept it in the kitchen.

Heidi grabbed a bagel and ran to the bus stop with Henry. Today was the deadline to choose a science experiment for the fair. She wanted

to find out what Lucy and Charlie had picked for their project. Heidi caught up with Lucy just before lunchtime.

"What are you and Charlie doing for the science fair?" Heidi asked.

"We're going to build a lemon battery that will light a Christmas tree bulb," said Lucy.

"A two-year-old could do THAT!"

said Melanie, who was listening in as usual. "You should call it 'Lemon Batteries for Babies.'"

"Mrs. Welli said our project was the hardest one of all," Lucy said.

"Who CARES?" said Melanie. "A volcano is WAY cooler than a battery made out of fruit. We're going to win, for sure."

Then Melanie did her famous twirl and walked off.

"What a stinkbug," said Heidi.

"You're not kidding," Lucy said. "How's it going with Stanley?"

"Okay so far," said Heidi as she reached into her cubby to grab her lunch bag.

"Wait—what's this?" Heidi asked. She stooped down to get a better look in her cubby.

Heidi pulled a bundle of grape Candy Pops from her cubby. The sticks were tied with a purple ribbon.

"These are my favorite!" said Heidi.

"I wonder where they came from," Lucy said.

"It must be Henry," said Heidi. "Yesterday, Henry ate the last grape Candy Pop, and I got really mad."

On the way to the cafeteria Heidi spied Henry in the school bus line. She waved the Candy Pops in Henry's face.

"Did you put these in my cubby?" Heidi asked.

"Why would *I* do that?" asked Henry.

"To be nice?" Heidi suggested.

"I'm not THAT nice," said Henry. "But can I have one?"

"In your dreams, bud," Heidi said, and she and Lucy continued down the hall.

In the cafeteria Lucy got in the hot-lunch line with Bruce. Heidi sat down with Charlie. They pulled out their sandwiches and water bottles.

"Want an oatmeal chocolate chip cookie?" Charlie asked. "I've got an extra."

"Sure," said Heidi.

Charlie handed her the cookie.

Then Lucy and Bruce set down their trays.

"It'll be tough to win the science fair," said Bruce. "All the second-grade classes in Brewster will be in it."

"What are YOU worried about?"

Lucy asked Bruce. "You're the smart-est scientist in the whole school!"

"Probably the whole state," said Charlie.

"Probably the whole universe," said Heidi.

"Thanks, guys," Bruce said. "But

it's not me I'm worried about. It's Melanie. I'm afraid that she's going to mess things up."

"I know what you mean," Heidi said.

They ate the rest of their lunch in silence.

Chapter 5

BUBBLES!

Mr. Heckelbeck's home laboratory had a kitchen and a library with bookcases from floor to ceiling. In the middle of the room was an island with a marble top and another sink on one side. This is where Heidi and Stanley set up their experiment.

Heidi's dad gave them each a white lab coat. Heidi set the supplies from the shopping bag on the island.

"Let's get started!" said Dad. "We need two quarts of water."

Dad handed a two-quart measuring

cup to Stanley. Stanley went to the sink and filled it with water. With Dad's help, he poured the water into the fishbowl.

"We need two-thirds of a cup of white vinegar," Dad said, pointing to

a red line on the measuring cup.

Heidi carefully poured the vinegar into the cup. The smell reminded her of dyeing Easter eggs. Then she poured the vinegar into the bowl.

"One tablespoon of baking soda," said Dad.

Stanley scooped a tablespoon of baking soda and smoothed it off with his finger. Then he dumped it into the bowl.

"Now for the raisins," said Dad.

Heidi dropped five raisins into the bowl.

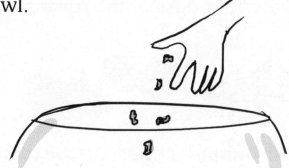

"It'll take a few minutes for the raisins to dance," said Dad.

"Why?" asked Heidi.

"Because something that's called a 'chemical reaction' is happening in the fishbowl," he said. "When you mix vinegar and baking soda, they make a gas called carbon dioxide—

that's what the bubbles actually are."

Heidi and Stanley watched bubbles form on the ridges of the raisins.

"The bubbles collect on the raisins and make them rise to the surface. When they get to the top, the bubbles pop and the raisins fall back to the bottom. Then it starts over again."

"There goes one!" said Heidi.

"There goes another!" said Stanley.

"Dad, can we add color to the water?" Heidi asked.

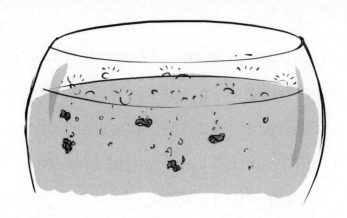

"Great idea," said Dad. He opened a drawer and pulled out a tray of food coloring.

"How about purple?" asked Heidi.

Stanley agreed, and Mr. Heckelbeck added a few drops of food coloring. The water turned a lovely shade of light purple.

"What if we added music?" said Stanley.

"A dance definitely needs music!" said Heidi.

"How about the Charlie Brown theme song?" suggested Stanley.

"Perfect!" Heidi said.

"I'll bring my dad's portable music player to the science fair," said Stanley.

"Cool," said Heidi. And then she had a thought: *Maybe the science fair won't be so bad after all.*

A SECRET MESSAGE

The next week of school flew by. Before they knew it, the science fair was a day away! Heidi was so excited that it was hard to concentrate on anything else.

"Math books, everyone!" Mrs. Welli said.

Heidi opened her desk and found, on top of her math book, a blank piece of paper with a happy-face border. The paper was crinkly in the middle, like it had been wet. Heidi sniffed it.

The paper smelled like lemons. It had a folded note attached to it with a paper clip. Heidi undid the paper clip.

A few scratch-'n'-sniff candy stickers floated to the bottom of her desk. *Can this be from my secret admirer?* wondered Heidi. Then she unfolded the note and read it.

Hold the paper with the happy faces close to a lightbulb and find a secret message.

"Hei-di!" called Mrs. Welli. "Kindly close your desk and pay attention."

Heidi shoved the note, the stickers, and the piece of paper inside her math book and closed the lid of her desk. Then she tried to work on double-digit subtraction, but she couldn't stop thinking about the note. *Who can it be from? Maybe it's Charlie Chen. Charlie's working on a lemon battery,*

and the paper smells like lemons. Plus Charlie gave me a cookie yesterday. It HAS to be Charlie!

During silent reading Heidi took her secret message—and a book—to the reading corner. She switched on a

lamp and held the paper to the light.
The message said:

Heidi quickly stuck the paper back inside her book and sat in the Comfy Chair. *I never knew Charlie liked me,* thought Heidi. *I'll have to thank him for all the cool stuff.*

In art Heidi tapped Charlie on the shoulder. He was molding a swan out of clay.

"I really liked your poem," said Heidi.

Charlie looked puzzled. "What are you talking about?" he asked.

"Didn't you leave a poem and stickers in my desk?" Heidi asked.

Charlie's cheeks began to turn red. "Huh?" he asked.

"Oh, uh, never mind," Heidi said. "Gotta go."

Heidi returned to her seat. *If Charlie isn't my secret admirer, then who can it be?*

There was one sure way to find out. . . .

Chapter 7

TRUTH POTION

Heidi pulled her *Book of Spells* out from under the bed. She opened to a chapter called "Truth Potions." *Here we go,* she thought. Heidi read a spell:

Who Is your Secret Admirer?

Have you been getting candy, notes, and gifts from a mysterious person? Are you the kind of witch who will go bonkers until you know who it is? Now you can remove the mask from your secret admirer with this simple spell.

Ingredients:
1 stick of peppermint gum
1 cup of cold water
2 drops of green food coloring

This spell must be cast in the presence of your secret admirer.

Hmm, Heidi thought. *My secret admirer has to be someone at school.*

I'll be with all my classmates on the day of the science fair—that should do the trick! Heidi looked at the next step.

Mix the ingredients in a bowl. Hold your Witches of Westwick medallion in one hand. Place your other hand over the mix and chant the following words:

ALACAZABRA!
ALACAZOO!
FIND OUT WHO
IS ADMIRING YOU!

Watch the name of your secret admirer appear in the potion.

This will be a breeze, thought Heidi. *I already have a pack of peppermint gum, and I can get water at school. All I need is green food coloring and a bowl.*

Heidi crept downstairs. She listened to make sure that no one was in the kitchen. She heard music coming from the study. *Mom must be working on her jewelry,* thought Heidi. Her mom had her own jewelry business.

Heidi tiptoed into the pantry and snooped through the baking supplies. She found a box of food coloring

and peeked inside. The green was missing. *Dad must have used it up on St. Patrick's Day,* thought Heidi. He had made green pancakes and green smoothies for breakfast. *Now what am I going to do?* she wondered.

Dad had food coloring in his lab, but his lab was off-limits. *Maybe I can mix colors like Mr. Doodlebee showed us in art,* thought Heidi. She set a small container on the counter and squirted yellow food coloring into it. She added two squirts of blue. Then she stirred it with her finger. The colors swirled into a beautiful shade of emerald green. *Perfect!*

Heidi snapped the lid back on and grabbed a plastic bowl and a spoon from the kitchen. Then she

snuck upstairs to her room and put everything into her backpack. *Wait! I almost forgot,* Heidi thought. She grabbed a stick of peppermint gum from her desk and dropped it into her backpack too.

Now I will find out who likes me once and for all!

Chapter 8

OH, HENRY!

On the day of the science fair Heidi carried her fishbowl into the Brewster Elementary gym. Her spell ingredients were safely hidden in her backpack. She was wearing her Witches of Westwick medallion, but it was tucked underneath her shirt. Dad carried the rest of Heidi's science experiment supplies in a shopping bag, and Mom held Henry's hand as she chatted with Aunt Trudy. Aunt Trudy rarely missed a family event.

A banner on the gym wall welcomed everyone. Tables with white table-cloths had been set up all around the room. The judges' table sat on a raised platform. The judges were Brewster's mayor, Lou Billings, and the editor of

Science Time! magazine, Clyde Jones.

Heidi found her table. It had a tent card with her name and Stanley's name in black curvy letters. There was also a white envelope with Heidi's name on it. *What's that?* she wondered. She set down the fishbowl. Dad placed a wooden stand on the middle of the table. Heidi covered

the stand with a white scarf and set
the bowl on top of it. She wanted her
experiment to stand out, so her dad
had helped her make a special stand.

"Looks great!" Dad said.

"Thanks," said Heidi.

Then she picked up the envelope

Heidi Heckelbeck
Stanley Stonewrecker

and turned away so no one would see what she was looking at. Inside the envelope she found a five-dollar gift card for Scoops ice-cream shop.

There was also a note:

Here's the Scoop!
I think you're cool!

From,
Your Secret Admirer

Heidi stuffed the note, gift card, and envelope in her backpack. When she looked up, Aunt Trudy winked at her. *Could Aunt Trudy be my secret admirer?* Heidi wondered.

She would have to find out later. Right now Heidi

needed to set up her science project. She and Dad went to the water fountain and filled the measuring cup with two quarts of water.

When they got back, Stanley had arrived with his portable music player and a sea-green poster. Fat paper letters

spelled DANCING RAISINS across the top. Stanley had drawn step-by-step pictures of how the science experiment worked. Note cards explained everything in words. He stood the poster on a stand beside the fishbowl.

Dancing Raisins

"That looks amazing," said Heidi.

"So does the fishbowl," said Stanley.

Stanley and Heidi got to work. They had to get the raisins dancing by the time the judges got to the table.

Henry peered into the fishbowl. "I

wike the poo-poo wah-wah," he said
with a mouthful of food. He really
meant "I like the purple water."

"What are you eating?" asked Heidi.
Henry swallowed.
"Raisins," he said.
Heidi grabbed the box of raisins
and looked inside. "OH NO!" she

shouted. "I can't believe it! You just ate the most important part of our science experiment!"

Heidi grabbed her brother's arm.

"Ow!" cried Henry. "What's the big deal?"

Dad pulled Heidi and Henry apart.

"Settle down," said Dad. "We can work this out."

"But he ruined our experiment!" wailed Heidi.

"Hold on," said Aunt Trudy, putting her hand on Heidi's shoulder. "I have an idea."

Aunt Trudy pulled out a tin of gumballs from her purse. "I always keep gumballs on hand," she said. "They keep me from snacking."

Aunt Trudy chose a few sour-apple gumballs from the tin. "These feel just like mothballs," she explained. "The carbon dioxide bubbles can collect on their surface too. So they'll also work in your experiment."

Heidi stared at the lime-green gumballs.

"But our project is called 'Dancing Raisins,'" said Heidi. "Not 'Dancing Gumballs.'"

"I can fix that!" said Stanley. "I brought my art supplies just in case."

"You did?" said Heidi.

Stanley nodded.

Heidi let out a sigh of relief.

"You know what?" she said. "I'm glad we're partners."

"Me too," said Stanley.

Chapter 9

KA-BOOM!

Plink!

Plink!

Plunk!

Heidi dropped the gumballs into the fishbowl. Stanley fixed the poster so it said DANCING GUMBALLS. Then he glued the word "gumballs" over the word "raisins" on all the note cards.

"I'm kind of glad that Henry ate the raisins," said Heidi.

"Me too," said Stanley. "Gumballs are cooler than raisins."

Henry ran up to the table. "The judges are walking around," he said.

Heidi spotted the judges at the first table.

"They won't get to us for a while," said Heidi. "Let's go look at the other experiments."

"Good idea," said Stanley.

Heidi and Stanley watched Lucy and Charlie show how a lemon battery works. They had five lemons with pennies, nails, and little cables attached to them. When they hooked up the cables to a tiny blue Christmas bulb, it lit up.

The judges clapped.

"Very well done!" said the mayor.

"I bet they'll win," said Heidi.

Stanley nodded.

Then they went to see Bruce and Melanie show off their volcano. The volcano sat on fake grass with mini plastic trees and houses all around it. Bruce was about to add the vinegar to the volcano when Melanie grabbed the bottle out of his hand.

"Let ME do it," said Melanie.

"Stop!" cried Bruce.

But it was too late.

Glug! Glug! Glug! Melanie poured half the bottle of vinegar into the volcano.

"Stand back!" shouted Bruce.

Everyone—except for Melanie—backed away from the table.

Ka-BOOM!

The volcano blew up. Melanie screamed as lava—which was really a stream of clay and bits of paper—splattered all over her face and clothes. A plastic tree hung from her long blond hair. Heidi, Lucy, and Bruce burst out laughing. Even Stanley laughed! Melanie clenched her fists and ran to the girls' bathroom.

"I'd say that was a huge success," said Bruce.

The judges frowned and wiped their sleeves.

DR. DESTRUCTO

Pop!

Fizz!

Boogie!

Stanley and Heidi's experiment was really in full swing once they were back at their table. The gumballs bounced up and down in the fishbowl.

"They're dancing like crazy!" said Stanley.

"Start the music!" said Heidi.

Stanley switched on the music player. The Charlie Brown theme song began to play. *Doo da doot doot, doo da doo . . . doo!*

Heidi Heckelbeck
Stanley Stonewrecker

"The gumballs look like they're really dancing to the music," said Heidi.

"It's magical," said Stanley.

"I agree," said the mayor, who had just arrived at their table.

The judges watched the gumballs dance to the music. They jotted some notes on their clipboards.

"What makes the gumballs dance?" asked the magazine editor.

"The music!" said Henry.

Everyone laughed. Then Heidi and Stanley took turns telling the judges what made the gumballs dance.

"Clever use of color," said the mayor.

"This is really great music," said

Principal Pennypacker as he snapped his fingers to the beat.

Then the judges moved on to the next table.

"Be right back," said Heidi.

Stanley nodded.

Heidi grabbed her backpack and raced to the water fountain. *Now's*

my chance to find out who my secret admirer is, she thought. She took the plastic bowl from her backpack and filled it with a cup of water. Then

she pushed open the door and stood in the hall. Heidi dropped a stick of gum in the bowl of water. Next she added two drops of the green food coloring and stirred it with a spoon. She put the bowl on the floor and stooped down next to it. Heidi pulled her medallion out from under her shirt and held it in her left hand. She placed her other hand over the mix and chanted the spell. The potion began to swizzle and swirl. Letters began to form in the fizzy green water.

Then—*wham!* The door to the gym banged into Heidi's back. She fell flat on her belly, and the potion spilled onto the floor before she could read the name.

"Ew, gross!" said someone behind her.

It was her brother, Henry.

"What are you drinking?" asked Henry. "Slime juice?"

Heidi jumped to her feet and grabbed her brother in a headlock.

Before she could really give it to him, the judges announced they had a winner. Heidi let go of Henry.

"Now come on, Dr. Destructo," said Heidi.

Heidi stuffed the bowl in her backpack and wiped up the mess with a paper towel.

Then they ran back inside.

Chapter 11

I KNEW IT WAS YOU!

"Thank you, second graders of Brewster!" said the mayor. "We're so proud of each one of you." Everyone clapped. "This year's winning science project showed both hard work and imagination. Principal Pennypacker, would you please open the envelope?"

Principal Pennypacker pulled a piece of paper from the envelope.

"The winners of the second-grade science fair are . . . Heidi Heckelbeck and Stanley Stonewrecker!"

Everyone clapped and cheered.

Heidi squealed and Stanley pumped his fist in the air. Then they jumped up and down and hugged.

"I never even dreamed we'd win!" said Heidi.

"Well, *I* did!" said Stanley.

"Will the winners please come to the judges' table and accept your award?" asked Principal Pennypacker.

Heidi and Stanley made their way to the judges' table. Kids high-fived them and whistled as they walked by. The mayor put a medal around Heidi's neck, and then he put another

one around Stanley's. The golden
medal had three pictures: a beaker,
a microscope, and the symbol of an
atom.

Wow, thought Heidi as she and
Stanley had their picture taken with
the judges and Principal Pennypacker.
I've never won a medal before. The
excitement made her forget all about
the ruined spell.

"It was fun being partners," said Heidi as she and Stanley walked back to their table.

"Yeah, it sure was," said Stanley.

"And now the party's OVER," said Melanie, who still had crusty lava spattered all over her clothes. Melanie grabbed Stanley by the arm. "Come on, Stanley. Your weirdo duties are over, and I need help with my stuff."

"See ya," said Heidi.

"See ya," said Stanley.

When Heidi got back to the table, Dad, Mom, and Aunt Trudy had already packed everything up.

Bruce walked over and tapped Heidi on the shoulder. "Congratulations, Heidi," he said shyly. Then he handed something to her. "This is for you," he said. "It's a lava candy dispenser. It shoots Red Hots out of the top." It was Bruce's latest invention.

"Cool," said Heidi.

She pressed a button and a red candy popped out.

"I should've known you were my secret admirer all along," said Heidi.

Bruce looked puzzled, but before he could answer, his mother steered him toward the door.

"Your grandmother is waiting," said Bruce's mother.

They hurried off.

I'm sure Bruce is my admirer, thought Heidi. *Who else can it be?* She hugged her fishbowl and headed out the door with her family.

On the other side of the gym, Stanley Stonewrecker watched Heidi disappear behind the swinging doors.

"Don't tell me you *like* her?" said Melanie as she turned and walked toward the doors.

"Nah, of course not," said Stanley— with a smile.

CONTENTS

Chapter 1

AN AWFUL TRUTH

Heidi Heckelbeck sat on the maple-tree swing and twirled the ropes together until they were tight. Then she lifted her feet and let the swing go. She spun round and round. Her thoughts were spinning as fast as the swing.

"You want to hear an awful truth?" asked Heidi as the swing unwound.

"I guess so," said her brother, Henry, who was sitting on the branch above her.

Heidi took a deep breath.

"Okay, here goes," she said. "I have no talent.

"I can't dance.

"I can't sing.

"I can't even act.

"I'm just a big fat nothing!"

"Well, *I'm* not," Henry said. "I've got talent."

"Like what?" asked Heidi.

Henry stood on the branch. He put one hand on the trunk and the other high in the air. "I am an ac-TOR!" he said.

Heidi rolled her eyes. "A BAD actor."

"No, a MIME actor," said Henry. "I can act out stories without talking."

"No words?"
Heidi asked.

"Not a one,"
said Henry.

"Really? This
I've GOT to see,"
said Heidi.

"Okay," said Henry as he jumped
out of the tree. "But I need a smooth
floor."

Heidi and Henry ran inside. Then
Henry hid behind the kitchen door.

"Ready?" asked Henry.

"Ready," said Heidi.

Henry moonwalked smoothly into

the kitchen. He had his hands in his pockets as his feet glided across the floor. He moved his head forward and back as he walked. One heel snapped to the floor in between steps. Then he stopped and looked around. His eyes got wide as he pretended to see something.

I wonder what Henry's looking at, thought Heidi.

Henry stooped and pretended to pick a flower. He pretended  to smell it. Then he picked another and another. When he had a whole bunch of pretend flowers, he walked

up to Heidi and offered them to her.

Heidi smiled and pretended to take them. "Very smooth, little dude," she said. "But it totally stinks."

"Why?" asked Henry.

"Because *you've* got talent and you're *younger* than I am."

"That's so silly," Henry said.

"I have to agree," said Mom, who had walked in during the show. "Everyone has talent. You just have to find something you like to do and practice it."

"But how am I going to do that?" asked Heidi. "There's only one week until the school talent show. That's not enough time to get good at anything."

"You can say that again," said Henry. "I've been practicing my mime act for months."

"See?" Heidi said. "It takes a *long* time to get good at something."

Mom sighed.

"You don't need more time or more talent," said Mom. "All you need is a good idea."

"Okay, fine," said Heidi. "I'm going outside to think."

Heidi pushed on the screen door, and it snapped shut behind her.

Just then Dad walked into the kitchen. "Did I miss something?" he asked.

EXCUSES, EXCUSES!

Heidi leaned against the maple tree and folded her arms. *How come Henry got all the talent in our family?* she wondered. *It's not fair.* Then Heidi spied a fat stick on the ground. She picked it up and poked at a knot in the tree. She hardly heard the back door

swing shut. Mom, Dad, and Henry had walked out into the yard.

"I've got something to cheer you up," said Mom. She set a tray of peanut butter cookies and a pitcher of milk on the picnic table.

Heidi continued to jab at the knot in the tree. It sounded hollow inside.

Maybe a squirrel lives in there, she thought. She stopped poking the tree. Heidi wished she could live inside a tree. *Then I wouldn't have to worry about being in a dumb talent show.*

"The cookies are still warm," said Dad, trying to get Heidi to the picnic table.

"And if you don't get over here, I'm going to eat yours all up," said Henry.

Heidi threw her stick on the ground. "Hey!" she barked. "Stay away from my cookies!"

"Oooh, I'm so scared," Henry said.

Heidi marched over to the picnic table, grabbed a cookie, and took a great big bite. *Mmmm,* she thought.

The warm, peanut-buttery goodness made her feel a teeny bit better.

"Maybe we can help you come up with an idea for the talent show," said Mom.

"Great idea!" said Dad. "Why don't you tell jokes? You're *very* funny."

"Too risky," Heidi said. "I might get booed off the stage."

"You could hula-hoop," said Mom.

"I can only do three twirls," said Heidi.

"Ride a unicycle!" Henry said.

"Too weird," said Heidi.

Heidi's family had more ideas—
baton twirling, magic tricks, a puppet
show, and reading poetry. But Heidi
had an excuse for everything.

"What are Lucy and Bruce doing?"
asked Mom.

"A skit," said Heidi. "They asked me
to join them, but I didn't want to."

"Why?" asked Henry.

"Because I'm not into acting," said Heidi. "Especially after I had to play the role of a scary apple tree in *The Wizard of Oz*."

"So you'd rather give up than try one of our cool ideas?" asked Henry.

"Pretty much," said Heidi.

A SHOW-STOPPER

Bruce Bickerson set down his lunch tray and sat next to Heidi.

"So?" he said.

"So, *what*?" asked Heidi.

"So, did you come up with an idea for the talent show?" asked Bruce.

Heidi dropped her carrot into her

lunch bag. Before she could answer, Melanie Maplethorpe, who never said anything nice to Heidi, answered for her.

"Didn't you hear?" said Melanie in a sugary-sweet voice. "Heidi can't be in the show because she's a weirdo with no talent."

Heidi looked at her peanut butter sandwich. Her cheeks began to burn.

"Very funny, Melanie," said Lucy Lancaster. "And I'll bet you have a showstopping number planned for the talent show?"

"Of course," Melanie said. "I'm going to perform an Irish step dance

that I made up myself. I've been taking lessons at the All-Star Dance Academy for four years. I'm pretty amazing."

Lucy rolled her eyes.

Bruce's mouth fell open.

Heidi stared at her sandwich.

"Well, see you around," Melanie said. She did her famous twirl and

walked off with Stanley Stonewrecker. Poor Stanley had to carry Melanie's lunch tray. He smiled weakly at Heidi, but she never looked up from her sandwich.

"Don't let Melanie bug you, Heidi," said Lucy. "The only thing SHE is good at is being mean."

But Melanie *did* bug Heidi. She made Heidi feel like the biggest weirdo on earth.

"I have an idea," Bruce said. "Maybe you could imitate Melanie for the talent show."

"You mean pretend to be Melanie onstage?" asked Heidi.

"Exactly," Bruce said.

Heidi smiled. "Been there, done that."

"Oh yeah!" said Bruce. "You were Melanie for Halloween!"

"How could we forget?" said Lucy.

"Well, I guess you can't do that again."

"Are you sure you don't want to do a skit with us?" asked Bruce.

"I'm sure," Heidi said with a sigh.

But Heidi wasn't sure about anything. Meanie Melanie's words had made Heidi feel worse than ever. Now she had to perform in the talent show just to prove she wasn't a weirdo—even though she felt like one. But what could she do?

285

Chapter 4

MAYBE?
MAYBE NOT!

"Boys and girls!" said Mr. Doodlebee, the art teacher. "Today I want you to paint a picture of your house. Add as many details as you can."

This sounds like fun, thought Heidi. *Maybe my talent is art.* Heidi painted her house frog green with crisscross shingles on the roof. Then she dabbed rosebushes with pink buds on either side of the front door.

Heidi liked her picture until she saw Natalie Newman's. Natalie's house had shutters and window boxes. She had even painted a porch with rocking

chairs, a flag, and a dog. *Wow,* thought
Heidi. *Natalie's picture should be in a
museum.*

Then Heidi looked back at her
own picture. Suddenly it looked like
a two-year-old had painted it. She
tossed it aside. *Looks like I have zero*

talent in art, she thought. *But who knows? Maybe I can do something sporty in the talent show. . . .*

Heidi decided to try her hardest in gym class. Everyone went outside and the teacher split the class into two teams for kickball. Heidi was up first. *I'm a good kicker,* she thought as she waited for the ball.

Stanley rolled the ball to Heidi. She kicked as hard as she could, but she missed and landed smack on her bottom. Melanie laughed in the outfield.

Heidi got up and tried again. This time Heidi kicked the ball good and hard. The only trouble was that Stanley caught it!

"Out!" shouted Melanie.

Heidi walked to the end of the line. Charlie Chen was up next. He kicked the ball over the fence and into the woods. It was an automatic home run. He ran the bases and high-fived Heidi and some of their other teammates.

Heidi sighed. *Looks like I stink at sports, too,* she thought.

In music, the class had solo tryouts for the winter concert. Heidi loved the theme: The Songs of Broadway.

"Are you trying out?" asked Lucy.

"I dunno," Heidi said. "Are you?"

"Definitely," said Lucy.

Heidi twirled her hair. *Maybe I should try out,* she thought. *Maybe my talent is singing. But what if my voice sounds funny? What if I throw up?*

Heidi's palms felt so sweaty just thinking about it.

She decided to watch some of her classmates try out first. Lucy walked to the front of the class and sang a song from *Annie*.

"Very good!" said Mr. Jacobs, the music teacher, as Lucy took her seat.

Eve Etsy went next.

"I'm going to sing 'My Favorite Things' from *The Sound of Music*,"

said Eve. When she finished singing, everyone clapped and whistled.

"Well done, Eve," said Mr. Jacobs. "You have perfect pitch!"

"Eve should be on Broadway," whispered Lucy.

Heidi nodded and slumped down in her chair.

After listening to Eve, Heidi decided not to try out for a solo. *Melanie's right. I have no talent,* she thought.

Chapter 5

RiSKY BUSiNESS

Heidi stopped at Aunt Trudy's on the way home from school.

Aunt Trudy was mixing some rosewater perfume for her mail-order business. "What's wrong?" she asked.

"Melanie said I have no talent."

"Do you believe her?" Aunt Trudy

asked while opening a bottle.

"Yes."

"But what does Melanie know about your talents?"

"Nothing," said Heidi. "But *I* know I don't have any talents."

"Of course you do."

"Name one."

"You're a good sister to Henry," said Aunt Trudy.

"Am not. I'm mean to him all the time. Next."

"You're a great baker," Aunt Trudy said. "What about those wonderful cookies you made for your school's cookie contest?"

"They were kind of a disaster."

"Oh . . . I had forgotten. Well, your cookies might have won if you had left out the cheese."

"Next," said Heidi.

"You're a fast runner."

"True. But what am I supposed to do with that? Run across the stage for my talent show act?"

Aunt Trudy laughed. "Heidi, you're impossible," she said.

"I know."

"Listen," said Aunt Trudy, "don't be so hard on yourself. I had no idea what my talents were when I was your age, but I figured it out in time. Besides, I'm pretty sure you have stage fright—and not a lack of talent."

"I think I have both," said Heidi. "How can I go onstage if there is a chance I might look stupid?"

"It's a risk you have to take."

"Ugh," said Heidi. But she knew Aunt Trudy was right. Heidi hugged her aunt and walked down the front steps.

"You'll come up with something," said Aunt Trudy. "You always do."

"I know," said Heidi. "But what?"

Chapter 6

TAP SHOES

Ka-thunk! Heidi heard a loud thump as she walked in the front door. *Whump!*

There it goes again, thought Heidi. The noise sounded like it was coming from the attic. Heidi closed the front door and ran up the stairs. Then she crept to the attic door and pulled it open.

"Hello?" she called into the rafters.

"Heidi? Is that you?" asked Dad.

"Yes, it's me," Heidi said as she ran up the stairs two by two. "What are you doing up here?"

"Looking for an old science book," said Dad. "It has a

formula for wax-bottle soda candy."

"What's that?" asked Heidi.

"It's liquid candy inside a mini soda bottle that's made out of wax. You bite off the top of the bottle and drink the candy syrup inside. I used to love them as a kid. Now I want to give them a jazzy new makeover."

"Sounds cool," said Heidi.

"It is," Dad said as he pulled a pair of black patent leather shoes from a box. He laughed.

"What are those?" asked Heidi.

"They're Mom's old tap-dancing shoes. Did you know she used to be a terrific tap dancer?"

"Really?"

"Miss Clickety Toes." Dad chuckled. He put the shoes in an empty shoe box lined with crinkly paper and handed them to Heidi.

Then Dad began to dig through another box.

Heidi stared at the shoes. They

looked just about her size. She turned them over. They had metal taps on the toes and heels.

"Wow," said Heidi.

"She sure had talent," said Dad. "And so do you!"

"No, not me," Heidi said. "I'm not good at anything."

"All you would need is a few lessons."

"I don't think so."

"What about mixing?" asked Dad. "You're great at mixing. We could mix up a tornado in an empty bottle."

"No, thanks. I need to find something that I'M good at."

"But you *are* good at science experiments. I would just be giving you a little help."

"Nah," said Heidi.

Then Dad pulled a dusty book from another box. It had a cracked leather cover with gold lettering. "Aha!" he said. He blew some dust from the cover. "Here's the book I've been looking for!" Dad hugged the book to his chest.

Then he looked at Heidi. "You should think about doing a science experiment for the talent show. It's okay to get a little help sometimes."

As Dad headed for the stairs, Heidi covered the tap shoes with the lid of the box and snuck them to her room.

Hmm . . . , she thought. *Maybe Dad's right—maybe all I need is a little help.* A smile spread across her face. . . .

Chapter 7

THE BRAVERY BUG

Heidi sat on her footstool and pulled off her sneakers. Then she wiggled her feet into her mother's tap shoes. They fit perfectly!

Heidi stepped in front of the mirror and tapped her toe on the hardwood floor. *Click!*

Then she tapped her heel. *Clack!*
Click! Clack!

This could be fun, thought Heidi.
She raced to her bed and pulled her
Book of Spells out from underneath

it. She looked up
"dance" and found
ballet, ballroom, jazz,
swing, and . . .

"Tap!" said Heidi out loud. She flipped to a spell called A Classic Tap Routine and read the directions.

A Classic Tap Routine

Do you have happy feet? Are you the kind of witch who likes to shuffle from one place to another? Does entertainment run in your family? Then this is the spell for you!

Ingredients:
1 cup of root beer
3 tablespoons of cranberry juice
1 teaspoon of sugar

Mix the ingredients in a tall drinking cup. Hold your Witches of Westwick medallion in one hand and place your other hand over the mix. Chant the following words:

Fizzy, Fizzy Wizzy!
Jazzy, Jazzy Zap!
Make This Witch an
Expert—
Help her Learn To Tap!

For a perfect routine,
drink the entire mix before
the performance. This spell
works instantly and lasts
up to two hours.

"Heidi!" Dad called. "Dinner!"

Heidi shoved her *Book of Spells* back under the bed. "Coming!" she yelled.

She pulled off the tap shoes and placed them back in the box. Then she slipped on her sneakers and smiled at herself in the mirror. *I'm going to rock this talent show!*

Heidi sat down at the table. "I'm so hungry I could eat a HORSE," she said.

"Would you settle for some turkey meatballs and spaghetti?" Dad asked.

"Yes, please!" said Heidi, holding out her plate.

Dad heaped her plate with meatballs and spaghetti.

"Wow," said Henry. "You sound happy. WHAT HAPPENED?"

"I'll tell you what happened," Heidi said as she sprinkled grated cheese on her pasta. "I finally came up with an idea for the talent show."

Henry slurped a piece of spaghetti.

"You did?" asked Mom.

"Yup," said Heidi.

"What are you going to do?" asked Henry.

Heidi thought for a moment. She didn't want to say she was doing

a dance, because they would all know that at this point it would take witchcraft to pull that off. Instead she said, "It's a surprise. You'll have to wait and see."

Henry rolled his eyes.

"This is very brave," Mom said. "Since when did you get so brave?"

"Today after school," said Heidi. "I kind of got tapped by the bravery bug."

Mom raised an eyebrow.

Heidi began to examine a meatball.

"Well, I think it's great," said Dad. "After all, we are a very talented family."

Chapter 8

WEiRDOS CAN'T DANCE!

The next morning at school Heidi stopped by the office on the way to her classroom.

"Oh hello, Heidi," said Principal Pennypacker. "Can I help you with something?"

"Yes," said Heidi. "I would like to

enter the school talent show."

"That's wonderful," said Principal Pennypacker. "What would you like to perform?"

"A dance," said Heidi.

"Any special type of dance?"

"No. Just a dance."

"I had no idea you could dance," said the principal.

"It's a hidden talent."

"Hmm. . . . I see." Then Principal Pennypacker looked Heidi in the eye and smiled. "You're always so full of surprises," he said.

Heidi laughed nervously. She often got the feeling that Principal Pennypacker knew she was a little different. *But he has no way of*

knowing that I am a witch, right?

At the end of the day, the talent show list was up! Everyone gathered around the bulletin board in the hallway to see the list of performers.

"Heidi! You signed up for the talent show!" said Lucy. "Why didn't you say anything?"

"I wanted to surprise you," said Heidi.

"Well, I'm *not* surprised," Lucy said. "I'm SHOCKED!"

"It's no big deal," said Heidi.

"Are you kidding?" Bruce said. "A few days ago you didn't want to have anything to do with the talent show!"

"Well, I changed my mind," said Heidi. "I'm going to do a dance."

"That's great," said Lucy. "What kind of dance are you going to do?"

"It's a secret," Heidi said.

"It's really *no* secret," said Melanie. "Weirdos definitely can't dance!" Then she burst out laughing.

Heidi balled up her fists at her sides. This time she would stand up to Melanie. Somehow she felt more confident now that she'd found a tap-dancing spell.

"Laugh all you want, Melanie," said Heidi. "My dance is going to be a BIG hit."

Melanie's jaw dropped. She wasn't used to Heidi standing up to her. She and her bobbing ponytail walked off.

"I'LL show her!" said Heidi.

"That's the spirit!" said Lucy.

And they slapped each other five.

Chapter 9

HAPPY FEET!

Heidi peeked out the window. Mom was gardening. She knew Dad was in the lab. Henry was upstairs practicing his mime act. *The coast is clear,* she thought. *Now I can make my potion.*

Heidi set a tall plastic Disney cup on the kitchen counter. Then she grabbed a bottle of root beer from the refrigerator. She poured one cup of root beer into the Disney cup. Then she pulled a cranberry juice box from the pantry shelf. Heidi added three tablespoons to the cup. Next she added the sugar and stirred everything together.

Heidi carried the potion to her bedroom and set it on her desk. *Now I need something to wear,* she thought.

Heidi searched through her closet. She chose a purple dress with sparkly swirls across the front. After getting dressed, Heidi slipped on Mom's old tap shoes.

Heidi looked at her kitty cat clock with the moving eyes and tail. *The talent show starts in an hour,* she thought. *If the spell lasts two hours, this would be the perfect time to cast the spell!*

Heidi grabbed her *Book of Spells* and put on her Witches of Westwick medallion. She held her medallion in one hand and placed her other hand over the mix. She had just begun to chant the spell when . . .

Rap! Rap! Rap!

Somebody knocked on her door! Heidi jumped to her feet and bumped

into her desk. Her potion tipped over. Heidi caught it with her free hand, but some of it sloshed onto her desk.

"Who is it?" asked Heidi. She quickly lay her jean jacket over her *Book of Spells* and medallion.

"It's Mom. We're leaving in fifteen minutes. Are you ready?"

"Almost!" said Heidi.

She listened to her mom's footsteps as she walked down the hall. *Phew!* she thought. *That was close!*

Heidi looked at the spill on her desk. Then she looked at the liquid in the cup. There was still a lot left. *This will have to do,* she thought. There wasn't enough time to sneak downstairs and make another batch.

Heidi chanted the spell and then chugged the mix. She scrunched up her face. *Yuck,* she thought. *That tastes gross.* Heidi wiped her mouth with the back of her hand and walked to the mirror to test the spell.

She tapped her toe on the floor. Her feet went *tappity-tap!* It was if they had been doing it her whole life. Heidi had to jump onto the rug to stop herself from dancing. *Wow,*

she thought. *This is even better than I imagined! I am not going to be a big nothing at the talent show after all. I'm going to be a STAR!*

Heidi stuffed the shoes back into the box, slipped on her sneakers, and zoomed downstairs.

"I'M READY!" she shouted.

Chapter 10

THAT'S A WRAP!

Heidi hopped into the car and sat next to Henry. He had on ankle-length black trousers, white socks, and black loafers. On top he wore a black-and-white-striped shirt, suspenders, white gloves, and a black top hat. Mom had painted his face pure white with red lips.

"You look like a REAL mime," said Heidi.

Henry gave the okay signal with his fingers. He was already in character.

"Are you all set with your dance?" asked Dad.

"I haven't seen you practice once all week," said Mom. "Are you sure you're ready?"

"Yup, all set," said Heidi, giving her shoe box a little kiss.

Dad dropped Heidi and Henry off at the back of the auditorium. Kids

had gathered outside the stage door. Heidi spotted Melanie. Her hair was all curled and she had on a flouncy Irish costume with a pink bodice and four layers of pink and white ruffles.

She looked like a real dancer. Heidi tried not to notice.

Mrs. Noddywonks, the drama teacher, handed out the program to the audience. Henry's act was first!

Soon Mrs. Noddywonks announced the first performer.

"Welcome, ladies and gentlemen, to the Brewster Elementary Talent Show!" she said. "For our first act we

have Henry Heckelbeck, who will be performing a mime routine."

Everyone clapped and cheered.

Heidi gave Henry a fist bump.

Then Henry moonwalked onto the stage. *Snap! Slide! Snap! Slide!* He seemed to float across the floor. Then

he performed his flower routine. When he offered the pretend flowers to Mrs. Noddywonks, the audience roared with laughter. Henry bowed and zoomed off the stage.

"Great job!" said Heidi.

"Thanks," said Henry. "I felt a little scared."

"It didn't show," said Heidi.

The next act was Charlie Chen who played the banjo. After him Natalie Newman told jokes. Then Mrs. Noddywonks closed the curtain so that Lucy and Bruce could set up their skit.

Lucy sat on a stool in front of the curtain and put her arms behind her back. Bruce stood behind her and slipped his arms through hers.

Nobody could see Bruce because he was behind the curtain. Then Lucy began to tell a story while Bruce did all sorts of funny things to Lucy with his hands. The crowd laughed and laughed as "Lucy's hands" slapped her face and scratched her head.

Then it was Heidi's turn. She took a
deep breath. Heidi walked under the
lights and tapped her toe on the stage.
Her feet began to shuffle. She tapped
across the floor one way and then
back the other way. She did digs, flaps,

and a move called the Cincinnati, which got a lot of claps and cheers.

But then . . . her feet suddenly stopped dancing! Heidi tapped the floor. Nothing happened. She tapped

again. Not one shuffle. *Oh no!* she thought. *The spell must've worn off!*

Heidi looked at the audience. People began to murmur. She tried to mimic what her feet and arms had been doing when she had been under the

spell. She could see her mom and dad in the audience. They knew she had used magic. Tears welled up in Heidi's eyes. *I'm going to be in big trouble,* she thought.

But Heidi was wrong. Her parents began to clap and whistle—and so did Aunt Trudy. The whole audience began to cheer! Heidi smiled and

quickly shuffled her way offstage.

"You were amazing!" Lucy said.

"How'd you pull that off?" asked Bruce.

"It wasn't exactly what I had planned," said Heidi, "but I'm glad everyone liked it."

"That was outstanding!" said Principal Pennypacker, who had been helping out backstage. "It was almost as if your feet had been bewitched!"

For a moment Heidi was speechless. *Does he know? But how? Nah, there's no way.* She thanked the principal and turned back to her friends.

Then Melanie pranced onto the

stage. She performed a perfect routine. Heidi wanted to barf.

"Your act was WAY better," Henry said.

Heidi spun around. "Thanks, little dude," she said. "But you know what? YOUR act stole the show."

"Really?" said Henry.

"Definitely," Heidi said.

After the last act, Heidi and Henry ran into the auditorium to find Mom, Dad, and Aunt Trudy.

Mom had a stern look on her face. Maybe her parents were a little mad after all.

"I'm sorry I used magic," said Heidi.

"That's cheating," said Mom.

"I know," said Heidi. "I just wanted to have a talent."

"Did you like tap-dancing?" asked Aunt Trudy.

"I loved it," said Heidi. "It made me want to get good at something."

"But you ARE good at something," said Henry. "You're good at getting in TROUBLE!"

Everyone laughed—even Heidi.

"I'd rather forget I have THAT talent," Heidi said.

"Bravo!" said Dad. "Now, who wants to get pizza and try out my new fizzy wax-bottle soda candy?"

"WE do!" shouted Henry and Heidi.

And they moonwalked all the way to the car.

Check out the next book starring

HEIDI HECKELBECK

"Oogie da boinga!" Heidi Heckelbeck said as she grabbed a chocolate chip cookie from the dessert plate.

"What's that supposed to mean?" asked Henry.

"Lucy told me about it," Heidi said. "It means 'wahoo!' at Camp Dakota."

An excerpt from *Heidi Heckelbeck Goes to Camp!*

"It also means you have camp spirit," said Dad.

An excerpt from *Heidi Heckelbeck Goes to Camp!*

"Well, I have oogie da boinga too," said Henry. "So why can't I go to sleepaway camp?"

"Because you're a SHRIMP," Heidi said.

"Am not."

"Are too."

"Soon Henry will be old enough for sleepaway camp too," Mom said.

"It's going to feel like FOREVER until I'm old enough," said Henry.

"Trust me," Dad said. "It'll go fast."

"And so will this evening if we don't hop to it," said Mom.

"You two go and pack," said Dad. "Henry and I will do the dishes."

Heidi and her best friend, Lucy Lancaster, were leaving for Camp Dakota in the morning. Lucy had gone to Camp Dakota last summer. Now Heidi and Lucy would get to go together for two whole weeks!

An excerpt from *Heidi Heckelbeck Goes to Camp!*

Heidi's clothes lay in piles on her bed. Mom had ironed name tags on to all of Heidi's belongings.

"Let's check off the last few things," Mom said.

"Okay," said Heidi.

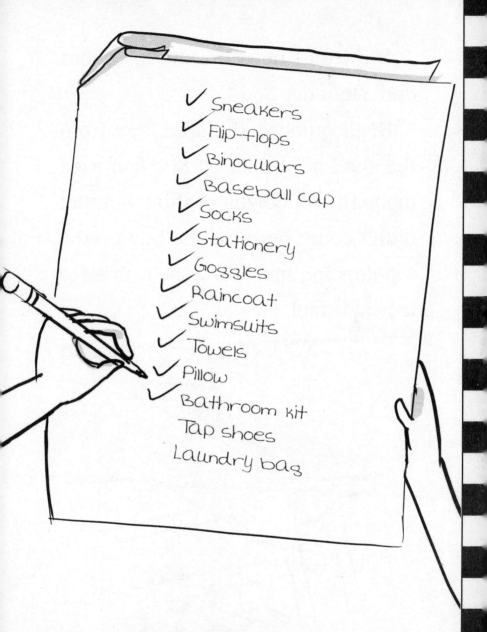

✓ Sneakers
✓ Flip-flops
✓ Binoculars
✓ Baseball cap
✓ Socks
✓ Stationery
✓ Goggles
✓ Raincoat
✓ Swimsuits
✓ Towels
✓ Pillow
✓ Bathroom kit
Tap shoes
Laundry bag

An excerpt from *Heidi Heckelbeck Goes to Camp!*

"Now all I need are my tap shoes and a laundry bag."

Heidi grabbed the shoe box from the shelf in her closet. She had tried tap in the school talent show, but that didn't count because she had used a tap-dancing spell. Now she wanted to learn for real.

Mom took one last look at the packing list. "I'll get you a laundry bag from the linen closet," she said.

As soon as Mom left the room, Heidi thought of something else she wanted to pack—something super-important. She kneeled on the carpet

An excerpt from *Heidi Heckelbeck Goes to Camp!*

and pulled her keepsake box out from under the bed. She opened the box and took out two things: her *Book of Spells* and her Witches of Westwick medallion. *Mom would never allow me to take these*, thought Heidi. *But what if there's an emergency?*

Heidi looked up and listened for her mom. Then she lifted a stack of clothes and carefully tucked her *Book of Spells* and medallion at the bottom of the trunk. She patted down her clothes as Mom walked back into the room.

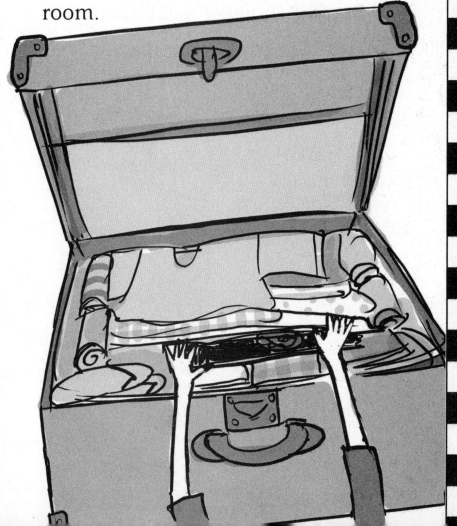

"That's it," said Mom, tossing a laundry bag to Heidi. "You're all packed for camp."

"Oogie da boinga!" said Heidi.

Then she shut and latched her trunk.